Kermit and Robin's Scary Story

by Michaela Muntean
illustrated by Tom Leigh

PUFFIN BOOKS

IMC
Centerville
Elementary School

For Madeline—M.M.
For Susanna—T.L.

PUFFIN BOOKS
Published by the Penguin Group
Penguin Books USA Inc., 375 Hudson Street, New York, New York 10014, U.S.A.
Penguin Books Ltd, 27 Wrights Lane, London W8 5TZ, England
Penguin Books Australia Ltd, Ringwood, Victoria, Australia
Penguin Books Canada Ltd, 10 Alcorn Avenue, Toronto, Ontario, Canada M4V 3B2
Penguin Books (N.Z.) Ltd, 182-190 Wairau Road, Auckland 10, New Zealand

Penguin Books Ltd, Registered Offices: Harmondsworth, Middlesex, England

First published in the United States of America by Viking,
a division of Penguin Books USA Inc., 1995

Published simultaneously in Puffin Books

1 3 5 7 9 10 8 6 4 2

Copyright © Jim Henson Productions, Inc., 1995

LIBRARY OF CONGRESS CATALOGING-IN-PUBLICATION DATA

Muntean, Michaela.
Kermit and Robin's scary story / by Michaela Muntean; illustrated by Tom Leigh.
p. cm. — (Viking easy-to-read)
Summary: Kermit the frog helps his nephew, Robin, write a ghost story.
ISBN 0-670-86106-5. — ISBN 0-14-037555-4 (pbk.)
[1. Authorship—Fiction. 2. Uncles—Fiction. 3. Puppets—Fiction.]
I. Leigh, Tom, ill. II. Title. III. Series.
PZ7.M929Ke 1995 [E]—dc20 95-14570 CIP AC

Printed in the United States of America
Set in New Baskerville

Reading Level 1.9

Contents

The Beginning of the Story

"The end," said Kermit.

He closed the book.

"Read it again," said Robin.

"It's my favorite story."

"I have a better idea," said Kermit.

"Let's write our own story."

4

"Our own story?" asked Robin.

"Yes. You tell it to me
and I will write it down,"
said Kermit.

"Okay," said Robin.

Kermit got a pencil and paper.

"We need a beginning," he said.

"How about *Once upon a time*?"
asked Robin.

"That's good," said Kermit.

"Once upon a time," Robin began,
"there was a frog named Shorty."

"One windy day,
Shorty was playing outside.
The wash was hanging
on the line to dry.

The sheets flapped in the wind.

The socks flapped in the wind.

The shirts flapped in the wind.

Shorty's shorts flapped in the wind."

"Flap, flap," said Kermit
as he wrote down the story.
"This is a silly story."

"No. It's a scary story," said Robin.

"Scary?" asked Kermit.

"Yes," said Robin. "Listen to this."

"All of a sudden
there was a big gust of wind.
It blew the wash off the line.

It blew the wash

into the deep, dark woods."

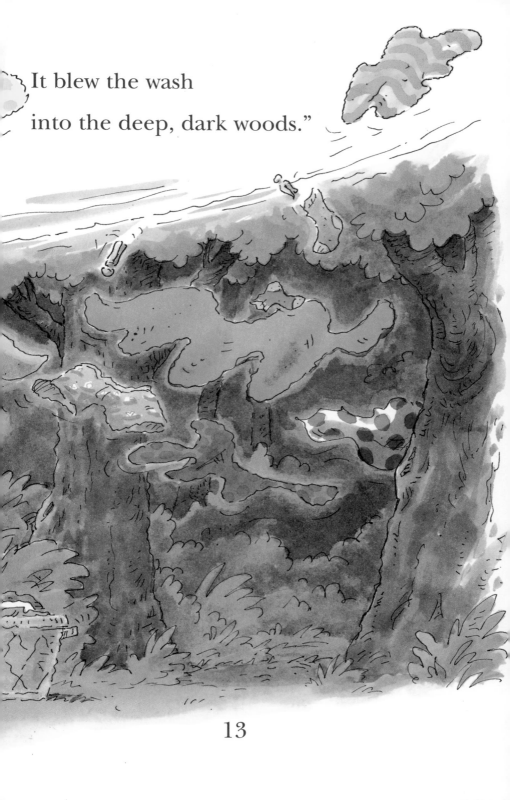

"'Oh, no!' cried Shorty's mother. 'My sheets, socks, shirts, and shorts are lost in the deep, dark woods!'

'I will save your wash,' said Shorty.

And he went off

into the deep, dark woods.

'You are very brave,'

said his mother."

15

"That is the beginning

of the story," said Robin.

"Do you like it?"

"It is a good beginning," said Kermit,

"good and scary.

What comes next?"

"The middle of the story," said Robin.

"Right," said Kermit.

"Ready?" asked Robin.

"Ready," said Kermit.

The Middle of the Story

"Shorty walked deeper and deeper
into the deep, dark woods,"
said Robin.
"He did not see
his mother's wash,
not even one sock.
But he did see a ghost."
"A scary ghost?" asked Kermit.
"A very scary ghost," said Robin.

"The very scary ghost
was big and white.
It flew through
the deep, dark woods.
Shorty was scared."

"He hopped into a tree.

He landed in a bird's nest.

Next to him

was a mother bird.

'My babies!' she cried.

'A ghost has taken my babies!

Please, help save my babies!'

cried the mother bird.

Shorty was scared.

'I'll try,' he said.

He peeked out from the tree

and looked at the ghost.

It was big and white and scary.

It was also covered

with little blue flowers."

"Shorty laughed.

'That's my mother's sheet,' he said.

He wasn't scared anymore.

Shorty hopped out of the tree.

He grabbed the sheet and pulled.

Four baby birds flew out.

'You are very brave, Shorty,'

said the mother bird."

Robin stopped.

"That was a great middle
of the story," said Kermit.

"Thanks," said Robin.
"Now I will tell you
the end of the story."

The End of the Story

"The birds helped Shorty
find his mother's sheets, shirts,
and socks," said Robin.
"They found the shorts, too.

Then the birds all flew
back to Shorty's house
and had a party.
Shorty was a hero."

"That night, Shorty's uncle
came to visit.
Shorty's uncle read
Shorty's favorite story to him
twenty-two times.

Then Shorty went to bed.
The End."

"Twenty-two times?" asked Kermit.

"Shorty has a nicer uncle

than you do, Robin."

"No," said Robin.

"No one has a nicer uncle than I do."

"Good night, Uncle Kermit."

"Good night, Robin."

The End